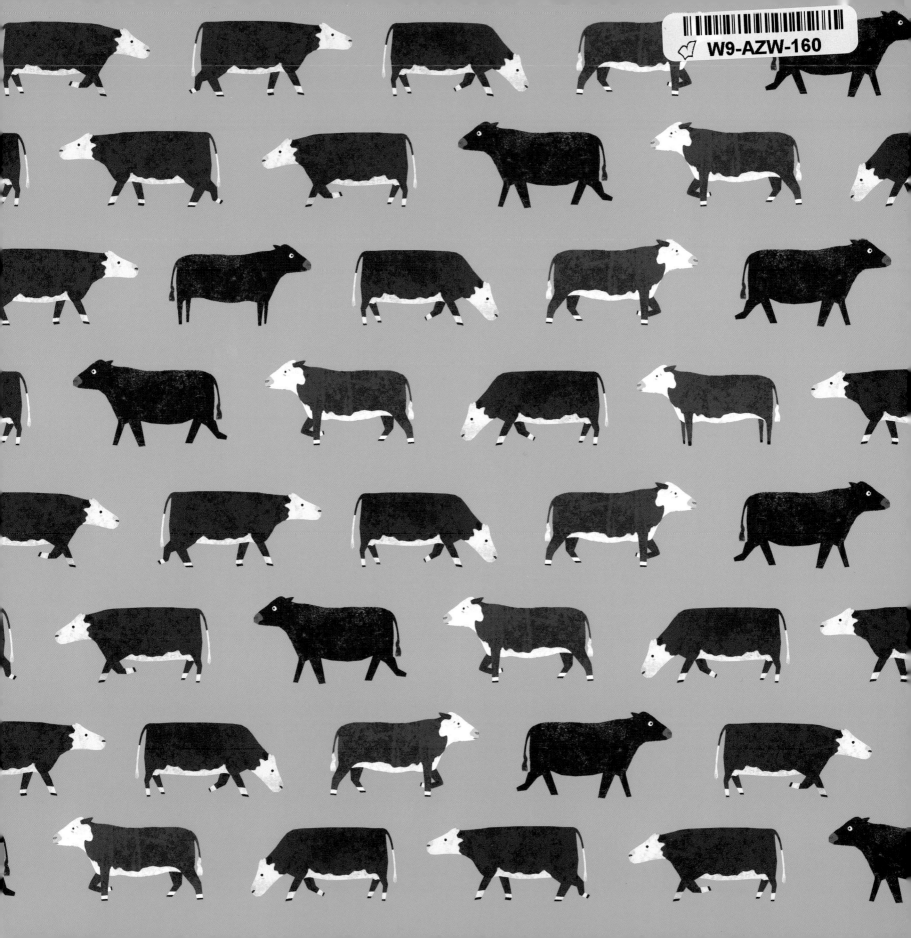

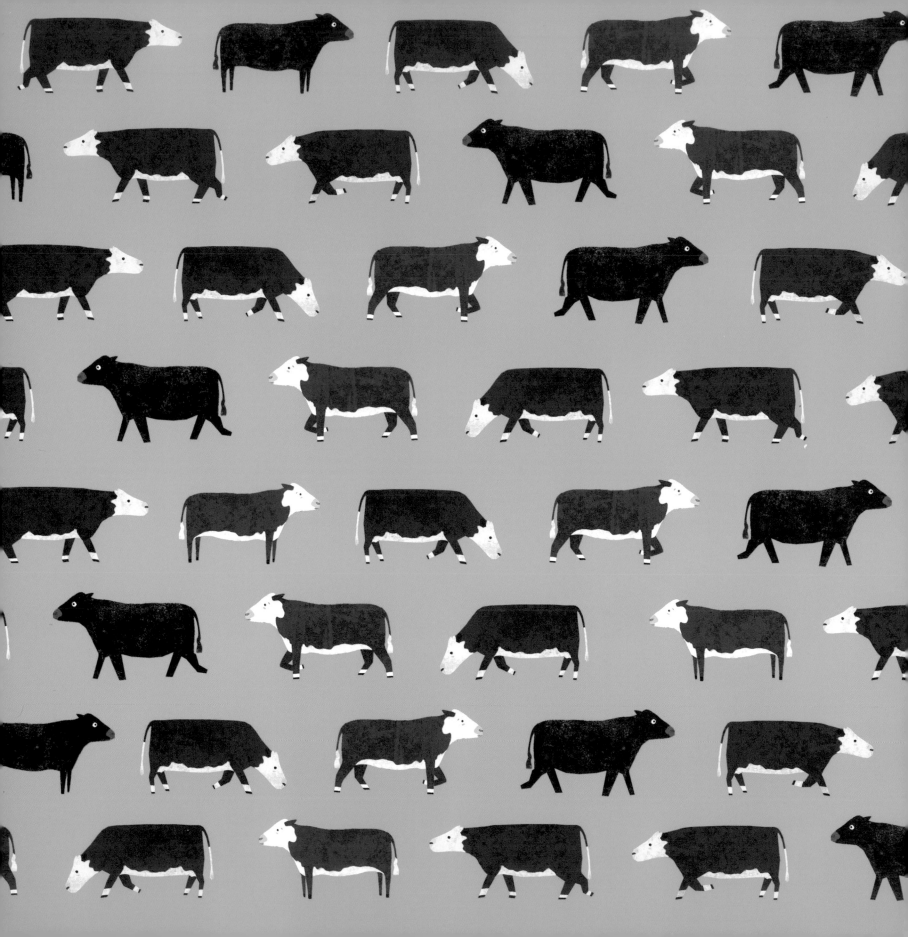

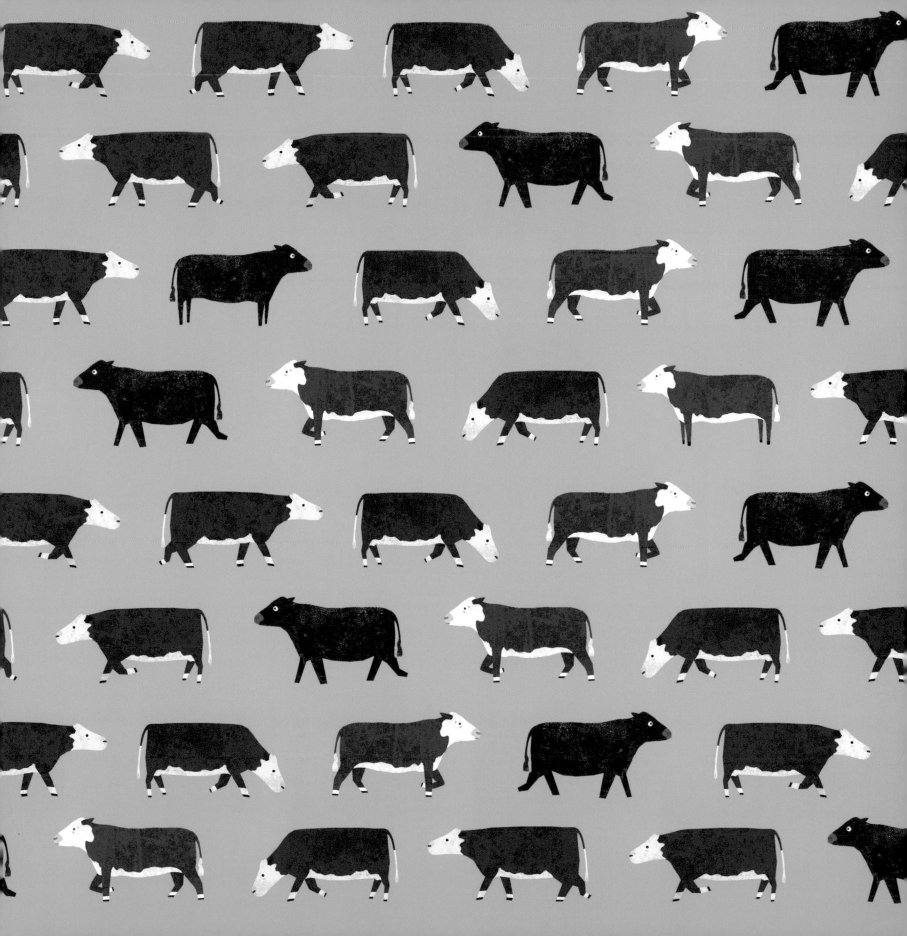

For every child who's ever felt alone.
- J.F.M

For Florence, and thank you Asia
for all your support!
- D.R.

LCCN 2016961448
ISBN 9781943147304 / 9781943147618

Text copyright © 2017 by Julia Finley Mosca
Illustrations by Daniel Rieley
Illustrations copyright © 2017 The Innovation Press

Published by The Innovation Press
1001 4th Avenue, Suite 3200, Seattle, WA 98154

www.theinnovationpress.com

Printed and bound by Worzalla
Production Date: October 2019
Plant Location: Stevens Point, Wisconsin

Cover lettering by Nicole LaRue
Cover art by Daniel Rieley
Book layout by Rose Clemens

ILLUSTRATED BY
DANIEL RIELEY

WRITTEN BY
JULIA FINLEY MOSCA

THE GIRL WHO THOUGHT IN PICTURES

The Story of Dr. Temple Grandin

If you've ever felt different,
if you've ever been low,

if you don't quite fit in,
there's a name you should know.

TEMPLE GRANDIN's that name.
In her tale, you'll find glory.

So, get ready, get set,
for this cowgirl's TRUE story.

In the city of Boston,
one hot summer day,

a sweet baby was born.
It was Temple! HOORAY!

Unique from the start,
an unusual girl,

she loved spinning in circles
and watching things twirl.

But some things she hated,
like certain loud sounds,

or bright, crowded places—
large cities and towns.

Frilly dresses with tags
made her itch, pull, and tug . . .

Something else that she hated?
A BIG SQUEEZY HUG!

A shy loner, this Temple,
but when she got mad,

when her feelings of stress
and frustration got bad,

quite a tantrum she'd throw—

KICK

HOLLER

BANG

SHRIEEEEEK!

Yet, still, by age three,
not one word did she speak.

"She'll never be normal,"
was what some did say.

"Her brain's not quite right.
You must send her away."

"AWAY? Not my Temple!"
her mother proclaimed.

"We will figure this out.
You should all be ashamed!"

Then, little by little,
though sometimes she balked,

special teachers helped Temple,
and one day, she TALKED!

And that thing with her brain . . .
it was AUTISM, see?

She was "DIFFERENT, NOT LESS,"
they all finally agreed.

COW

Like most kids her age,
she loved ice cream and art,

but the way Temple THOUGHT—
that's what set her apart.

If something was mentioned,
for instance, a FLY,

in her mind, she'd see dozens
of PHOTOS buzz by.

When the time came for school,
let's just say that was hard.

Kids taunted and chased her
all over the yard.

They picked on poor Temple—
how CRAZY it drove her.

They teased her for saying things
over and over.

And over . . .

LOOK
AT
HER!

And over . . .

AND over.

Until finally, she SNAPPED!
Yes, she did, lost her cool—

threw a book at a kid
and was kicked out of school!

No one really GOT Temple,
but well, then again . . .

The truth of it was,
Temple didn't get THEM.

"You need time away,"
said her mom. "That's what's best.

You'll go visit your aunt
on a ranch way out west."

And guess what? Fitting in
on a farm WAS less stress,

since the PIGS didn't care
if her hair was a mess.

Quite a sweet spot, she had,
for the cows in their herds,

such big, gentle beasts,
who knew nothing of words.

As she watched her new friends,
a thought popped in her head:

"These cows think like ME—
in PICTURES instead!"

At a NEW school that fall,
Temple found more support

and a teacher who taught her:
"You'll never fall short

when you find what you're good at,
like science—you'll SOAR!"

And that teacher was right.
He had opened a door.

So, she built a machine
like she'd seen on some farms,

an INVENTION that hugged her
with boards, and not arms.

IT WORKED! She had done it—
from memory, it's true.

And just like the cows,
it made Temple calm, too!

"I'm SPECIAL," she thought,
"like a bright shooting star.

My attention to details
could help me go FAR!"

Through her studies, she learned
there were farms not so kind.

"I will help them," she said.
Some SOLUTIONS, she'd find.

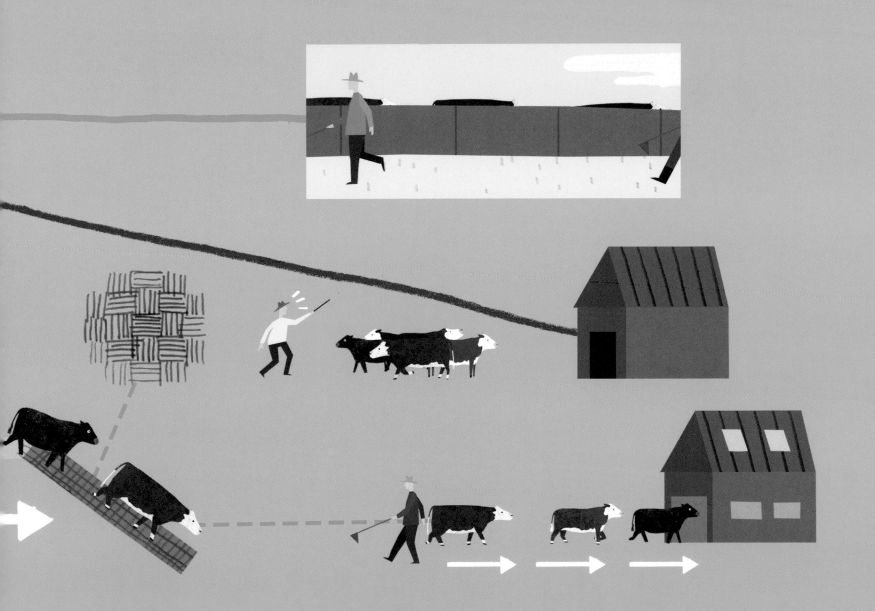

And then, something COOL . . .
Can you guess? Could it be?

Off to COLLEGE she went!
A degree? She earned THREE!

And though ladies weren't experts
on farms at that time,

do you think that stopped Temple?
NO WAY! She did fine.

She stepped through that door
and went FORWARD. No tears.

She took on the world,
but at times, she had fears.

Because some things were SCARY,
like people she'd meet

who'd ignore her ideas
and, well, wouldn't be sweet.

But she never gave up,
learned her stuff through and through,

like why cattle will circle
and what makes them MOOOoooooooo.

To build better farms
was her goal—she would do it.

"Be KIND to our creatures.
They have FEELINGS!" She knew it.

And slowly but surely,
she changed many minds,

until farm after farm built
her AWESOME designs!

Word spread about Temple,
her feats not so small.

"Temple Grandin? She's grand!
SHE'S THE GRANDEST OF ALL!"

LIVESTOCK HANDLING
AND TRANSPORT

BY TEMPLE GRANDIN

Now, for these things and more,
she's won honors and prizes.

And a MOVIE was made!
But the BIGGEST surprise is . . .

that girl with the future
that couldn't be bleaker?

Yes, the once-silent girl . . .
she is now a big SPEAKER!

Today, she spreads hope
with her stories and speeches.

From NEW YORK to SYDNEY
to ROME, Temple teaches:

"Each person is special—
so UNIQUE are our minds.

This world needs YOUR ideas.
It takes brains of ALL kinds!"

So, here is the lesson:
Feeling odd or offbeat?

Being DIFFERENT might just
be what makes you so NEAT!

Don't let doubt hold you back,
not for one minute more.

STAND TALL, and like Temple,

MARCH RIGHT THROUGH THAT DOOR!

Dear Reader,

As a child, I was really glad that my mother always encouraged my ability in art. I encourage you to find something you are good at and work on developing it.

If you are interested in becoming a scientist like me, find cool new ways to look at things such as microscopes and telescopes. Explore nature. Think up your own hands-on science experiments.

Keep learning, especially from your mistakes.

Temple Grandin

FUN FACTS AND TIDBITS FROM THE AUTHOR'S CHAT WITH TEMPLE!

A Spaced-Out Childhood

"If it flew, I loved it!" Temple said, when asked about her childhood hobbies. "As a little kid, I worshipped astronauts." In addition to playing with kites, airplanes, and spaceships, she was also fond of drawing. "I'd have been lost in school without art class," she said. During her teenage years, Temple developed a new passion for television shows like *Men into Space*, *The Twilight Zone*, and *The Man from U.N.C.L.E.* "I was a total Star Trek fan," she admitted. Her favorite character? Mr. Spock, of course—a lovable half-human who often had trouble relating to certain emotions.

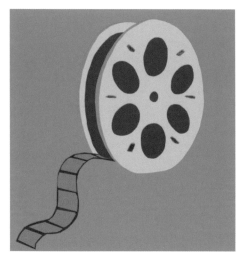

A Real Cowgirl Mooooovie

Only a few people in the world can say they've been the subject of a Hollywood movie, and Temple is one of them! In 2010, HBO released *Temple Grandin*, starring actress Claire Danes, who won a Golden Globe Award for her role as the well-known scientist. The docudrama focused on Temple's early life with autism and her long, accomplished career in the livestock industry. "I loved the fact that my actual drawings were in the movie," she said, referring to the blueprints for her inventions. Temple said she was also glad that the film included the three most important people in her life: "All the main characters in the movie, Mr. Carlock, Aunt Ann, and Mother, were shown very nicely."

A Signature Look

When you picture Temple Grandin, one item of clothing probably comes to mind: cowboy shirts! Over the years, the famous animal scientist has built up an amazing collection of the tops, which she often likes to pair with one of her signature scarves. But Temple didn't always have such a confident and unique sense of style. "I had people who told me I did have to clean it up," she admitted. As a child and young adult, she hated dressing up, especially in anything itchy. When she discovered cowboy shirts (which she prefers to wear over a soft cotton T-shirt), they just worked, and today it's hard to find her in anything else. In 2011, Temple even wore her trademark look to the prestigious Golden Globe Awards ceremony in Hollywood!

A Woman in a Man's World

Ask Temple about working on farms as an animal scientist in the 1970s, and the answer might surprise you. "That was worse than the autism was . . . much worse," she said. Even with all the obstacles she faced as a child and teen, Temple said her greatest challenge in life was "being a woman in a man's world. That was not easy." She added that during that time, "the only women working in Arizona feed lots were secretaries in the office." So what kept Temple going when the odds seemed stacked against her? "I wanted to prove to people that I was not stupid, that I could do it. And *that* motivated me."

A Doorway to the Future

A study of Temple's journey would not be complete without the mention of doors. You see, for Temple, they aren't simply a way to get in and out of a room, but a symbol of what's to come. "In order to think about something abstract like my future, I have to have something I can actually visualize, like a door," she explained. Temple said she first came up with the idea as a young girl, when the suggestion of moving on to new experiences or places could be frightening. Picturing herself stepping through a doorway helped ease some of that anxiety. "That's the way I thought about everything," she admitted.

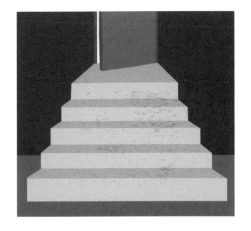

A Wordy Accomplishment

Who would believe that a girl who didn't speak as a small child would someday travel the world as a famous speaker? If you've heard one of Temple's captivating lectures, then you know it's possible. Still, spreading her message in front of large crowds didn't always come easily.
"I wasn't a good public speaker when I first started," she admitted. "When I was in graduate school, I panicked, and I walked out of my first talk." So how did she get so good? A lot of practice and one particular secret weapon: "I made sure I had really good slides to cue me," she explained. "I was an awkward speaker, but I had fantastic slides!"

Photo courtesy of Temple Grandin

1947 Born August 29th in Boston, Massachusetts

1950 Diagnosed with brain damage (quickly recognized as autism)

1961 Spends summer on her Aunt Ann's ranch in Arizona

1961 Starts Hampshire Country School and meets Mr. Carlock

1970 Earns psychology degree from Franklin Pierce College

1973 Begins writing articles as livestock editor for *Arizona Farmer-Ranchman*

1975 Earns master's degree in animal science from Arizona State University

1989 Earns doctoral degree in animal science from University of Illinois

1951 Begins to speak with help from tutors and speech therapy

COW

1961 Expelled from school for bad temper

1965 Invents her squeeze machine

1985 Speaks publicly for the first time at Autism Society of America conference

1976 Invents curved chute system for cattle

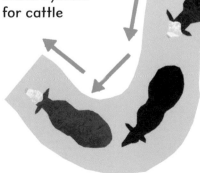

1990 Installs first center track restrainer system for livestock

2010 Named a fellow by the American Society of Animal Science

2010 Becomes subject of HBO award-winning movie, *Temple Grandin*

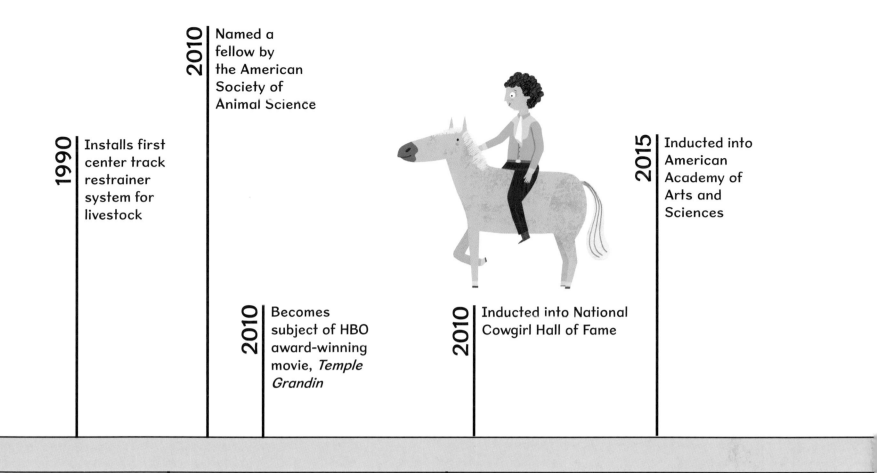

2015 Inducted into American Academy of Arts and Sciences

2010 Inducted into National Cowgirl Hall of Fame

Writes first *New York Times* bestseller, *Animals in Translation*

2005

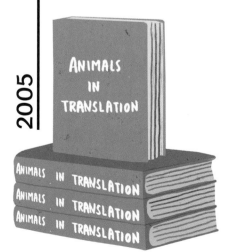

2010 Named one of *Time* magazine's 100 most influential people

Lives in Fort Collins, Colorado (professor of animal science at Colorado State University)

Present Continues to write, speak, conduct research, and teach about animal science and autism

ABOUT DR. TEMPLE GRANDIN

Dr. Mary Temple Grandin (fondly known as Temple) was born on August 29, 1947, in Boston, Massachusetts. Despite facing many obstacles throughout her life, Temple has made it her mission to educate the world about two things: the importance of treating animals with compassion, and autism, a condition affecting millions worldwide, including herself.

At the age of two, when she still hadn't begun to speak, Temple was mistakenly diagnosed with brain damage. It quickly became clear, however, that she had autism: a complex disorder of brain development that can affect a person's ability to communicate. In those days, many doctors thought children like Temple could not be treated and therefore recommended sending them away to live in special homes. Fortunately, Temple's mother, Eustacia Cutler, took her to a neurologist who recommended speech therapy.

With assistance from special teachers and nurses, Temple finally began to speak around the age of four. Still, she found it challenging to stay focused on certain tasks and to control her frustration in stressful situations. Like many people with autism, making conversation with friends, reading facial expressions, and even understanding the importance of hygiene and grooming did not come naturally to Temple. These differences made it quite difficult for her to fit in with classmates at school. When she was fourteen years old, she lost her temper and threw a book at a student who was teasing her. Unfortunately, she was asked to leave the school and not return.

The summer following that dismissal marked a major turning point in Temple's life. She spent a few months living and working on her Aunt Ann's ranch in Arizona, where she developed a deep connection with animals. She was especially fond of cows and quickly realized they were visual thinkers. Like her, they noticed details about their surroundings that many people did not. Although Temple has always been careful to point out that not everyone with autism is a visual thinker, she has often described herself as someone who "thinks in pictures."

When she returned from Arizona, Temple began attending a new school, Hampshire Country School in New Hampshire. It was there that she met William (Bill) Carlock, a teacher and former NASA scientist who would become her lifelong friend and mentor. He immediately recognized that the fifteen year-old had an unusual talent for remembering images, much like a computer is able to retrieve stored photos. Mr. Carlock encouraged her to use this special gift to her advantage. She also credits him with helping her develop a real interest in science.

During her senior year, under Mr. Carlock's guidance, Temple built her first official invention: the squeeze machine (sometimes called the hug machine). It was based on a device that she saw on the farm—a pressurized chute that kept cows calm during their vaccine shots by gripping them in a nice firm manner, much like a strong hug. Even though Temple did not like the sensation of being hugged by people, she found that she craved and appreciated the sense of calmness her machine brought her.

After high school, Temple began attending college, something that many people thought would never be possible because of her autism. At Franklin Pierce University (called Franklin Pierce College at that time) in New Hampshire, she continued to work on her squeeze machine. It took a lot of convincing, but the school allowed her to conduct a research study, in which she observed the way students felt before and after using the device. Projects like this eventually led Temple to realize what she wanted to do with her life: study the behavior of farm animals and use what she learned to improve the way they were treated. Her hard work and dedication to this goal enabled her to earn three degrees, including a PhD in animal science.

Even with her impressive education, Temple still had a hard time getting her voice heard in the farming industry. Her career began in the 1970s, a time when hardly any women were experts in the field. But Temple was persistent. She continued to push her way onto farms, ranches, and meat processing plants, writing many articles for well-known livestock magazines and publications. Years of research led her to conclude that the way animals, especially cows, were transported and handled often caused them a lot of pain, stress, and fear. Temple noted that many cows were injured as they were moved from place to place on steep, slippery ramps in poorly lit facilities. She believed that such rough and careless treatment was unnecessary and cruel, even for those being raised only for their meat. Eager to improve things, Temple decided to put herself through some of the harsh processes many cows endured on a daily basis, using her own animal-like intuition to see and feel things as they did. The most important findings of her experiments included the notion that cows prefer solid pen and chute walls to open fencing, which leaves them susceptible to loud sounds, frightening shadows, and other undesirable distractions. They also like well-lit areas and are often reluctant to enter tight, dark spaces or buildings.

Using the data she collected, Temple was able to invent ways to make transporting safer and more comfortable for livestock. Among her most valuable contributions as an animal scientist are two inventions: the center track restrainer system, used to hold animals in a gentle upright position on the conveyor belt, and the curved loading chute depicted in this book. Temple developed the latter after observing that herds prefer to move around their handlers in a circular pattern; it keeps them calm. Her new and improved design employs solid walls and non-slip floors, both of which keep cattle from being spooked or injured as they move calmly through a curved walkway in single file. In addition to these innovations, Temple also created an important evaluation method to ensure that major meat plants and retailers treat their animals with dignity. Today, a large percentage of the world's meat producers use her compassionate systems and procedures.

Equally as important as her work with animals are her contributions to the autism community. Temple now travels the world to tell her story and inspire others. It is her belief that children with autism need early intervention and a good support system to motivate them. Much like her mentor Mr. Carlock, she believes that encouraging children to find their own unique strengths is often the key to their success.

Throughout her long career, Temple has received many prestigious awards and honors, including being named a fellow by the American Society of Animal Science and her induction into the American Academy of Arts and Sciences. As a prominent speaker, she has appeared on a number of popular television shows, and as an author of numerous books, she has twice landed on the *New York Times* Best Seller list. In 2010 alone, she was inducted into the National Cowgirl Hall of Fame, *Time* magazine named her one of its 100 most influential people, and HBO produced *Temple Grandin*, an award-winning movie about her life.

Photo courtesy of Temple Grandin

Today, Temple lives in Fort Collins, Colorado, where she admits that her biggest passion in life is her work—making a difference as an advocate for people with autism and for animals. She continues to speak, write, and conduct research about both topics, even finding time to teach as a professor of animal science at Colorado State University.

One quote often attributed to Temple is: "I am different, not less." It is quite possibly the perfect way to describe her feelings about life with autism. Although some people might not understand, Temple has said that even if a cure were available, she would not wish to be cured of her autism. Without it, she believes she may not have become the AMAZING SCIENTIST she is!

Acknowledgements

The publisher, author, and illustrator are immensely grateful to Dr. Temple Grandin for contributing personal photos, speaking at length with the author, and providing helpful commentary throughout the creation of this book.

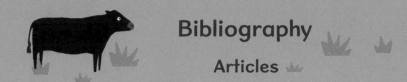

Bibliography

Articles

"Temple Grandin Biography.com." *The Biography.com*. A&E Television Networks, April 2, 2014. http://www.biography.com/people/temple-grandin-38062.

Sacks, Oliver. "An Anthropologist on Mars." *The New Yorker*, December 27, 1993. http://www.newyorker.com/magazine/1993/12/27/anthropologist-mars.

Grandin, Temple. "Temple Grandin on a New Approach for Thinking about Thinking." *Smithsonian.com*. Smithsonian Magazine. July 2012. http://www.smithsonianmag.com/science-nature/temple-grandin-on-a-new-approach-for-thinking-about-thinking-130551740.

Videos/Film

"In Depth with Temple Grandin." *C-SPAN Book TV*. C-SPAN video. November 1, 2009. http://www.c-span.org/video/?289706-1/depth-temple-grandin.

"The World Needs All Kinds of Minds." *TED2010*. TED. February 2010. http://www.ted.com/talks/temple_grandin_the_world_needs_all_kinds_of_minds.

Temple Grandin. Dir. Mick Jackson. HBO Films, 2010. Film.

Books

Grandin, Temple, and Richard Panek. *The Autistic Brain: Thinking Across the Spectrum.* New York: Houghton Mifflin Harcourt, 2013. Print.

Schopler, Eric and Gary B. Mesibov, eds. *High-Functioning Individuals with Autism.* New York: Springer US, 1992. Print. Current Issues in Autism.

Grandin, Temple. *Thinking in Pictures: My Life with Autism.* New York: Doubleday, 1995. Print.

Grandin, Temple and Catherine Johnson. *Animals in Translation: Using the Mysteries of Autism to Decode Animal Behavior.* New York: Scribner, 2005. Print.

Website

Temple Grandin, PhD
http://www.templegrandin.com

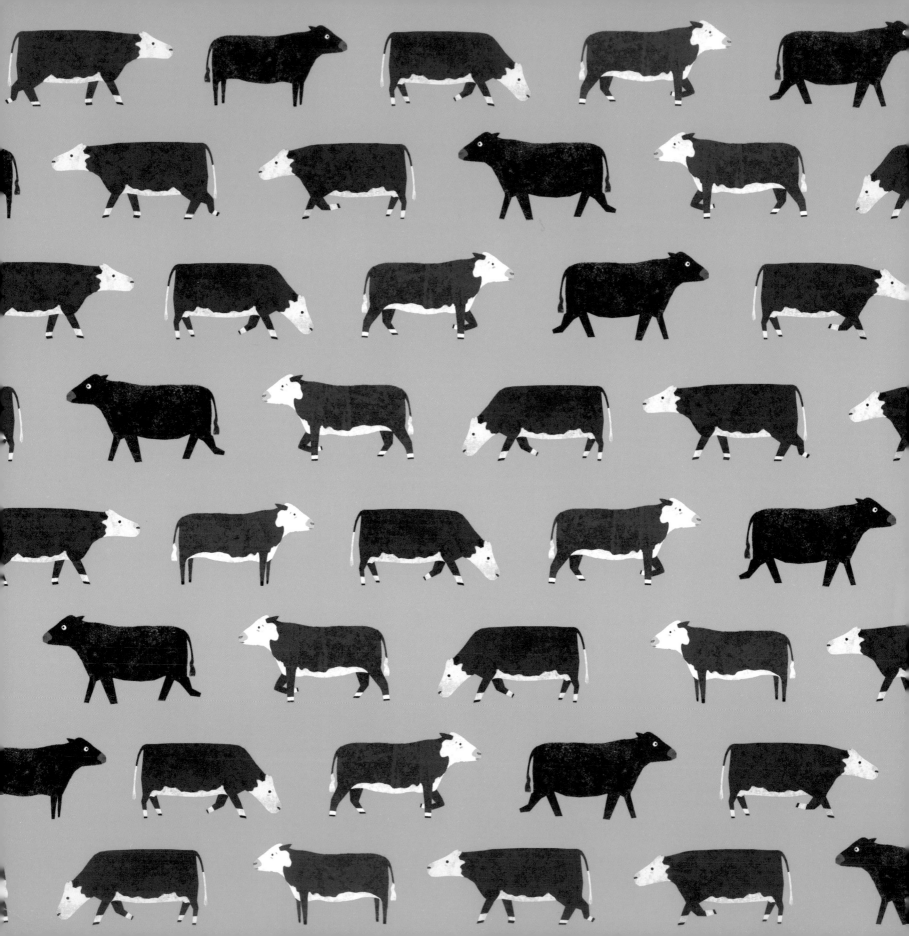